Mermaid Mysteries

Rosa
and the
Water Pony

Written by **Katy Kit**

Illustrated by Tom Knight

Boxer Books

To Anna,

my very own water baby.

Contents

Smugglers' Cove

Coral Reef

Crystal Grotto

Rocky Ride

Watery Downs

Merschool

CHAPTER 1

The Crystal Grotto

With a flick of her tail, Rosa dived into the water. Melody, Sula and Jasmine stared at the bubbles on the surface, waiting for her to reappear. Soon enough, Rosa's head popped out. "Race you to Crystal Grotto,"

she called, "last one there's a sea slug!" And, with another flick of her tail, she was gone.

Splish.

Splash.

Splosh.

Quickly, the other three mermaids leapt in after her.

9

Soon, all four were speeding through the water, swishing their tails up and down as fast as they could. Rosa got there first – she always did – then Sula, then Jasmine, then Melody.

"Bad luck, Melody," said Jasmine. "Looks like you're the sea slug."

"Only because you knocked off my glasses with your crazy swimming," said Melody.

"I couldn't see a thing!"

"Hey, you two," called Rosa, who was floating outside Crystal Grotto with Sula. "Come over here and read this."

Crystal Grotto was a small underwater cave, right in the middle of Mermaid Bay. It was the place where everyone came to meet friends and to find out what was going on. Outside, someone had pinned up a large poster. The mermaids crowded round to read it.

This is what it said:

Mermaid Bay's

10th Midsummer Carnival

On Saturday, 30th June, at 12 pm prompt there will be a procession from Crystal Grotto to King Neptune's Palace. A prize will be awarded to the team with the most spectacular display.

All entrants welcome!

"That's this Saturday," said Rosa. "I've heard the prize is to be awarded by King Neptune himself. And," she

continued, leading them inside, "take
a look at what it is."

Sula,
Jasmine
and Melody
gasped.
There,
gleaming
in the
darkness, laid out
between the two halves of a giant
clam's shell was the most magnificent,
the most wonderful, pearl necklace
any of them had ever seen.

Now, mermaids, especially young

13

mermaids, just love jewels. They can't help it. They're just made that way. So, as soon as Sula, Melody and Jasmine saw the necklace, they all had the same thought: they just had to win.

"OK," said Rosa. "Let's get organised. We'll need to enter as a team. I've thought of a name. What about 'The Waterbabes'?"

The mermaids giggled.

"Well, we probably will be the youngest team," said Melody.

"As for the display," Rosa continued, "if we can find a friendly sea horse, we could use some mermaid magic and—"

"Turn it into a water pony!" interrupted Jasmine.

"Exactly," said Rosa. "I've been practising my finflips and tailspins all week.

I'm sure I could perform them on horseback. It'll look stunning."

"That's a brilliant idea, Rosa!" said Sula.

The mermaids sat down on the seabed to think of ways to dress up.

"The seagulls have collected some lovely pieces of coloured gauze. I'll ask if we can use them to make scarves," said Sula.

"And
I could
find out if the
water fairies will
let us borrow some of their golden
ribbons," suggested Jasmine. "They
look so pretty fluttering about in the
water."

The mermaids were so excited, they

didn't notice they were being watched.

"You don't stand a chance," said
a loud voice.

The mermaids looked round. The
voice belonged to Myrtle, an older
mermaid they knew from Mermaid
Bay Merschool. She was with her twin

sister Muriel,
sitting on a
rock. They
were always
being mean
to the
younger
girls.

"How old are you? Nine, ten? And you think you can win?" she sneered.

"Ignore them," whispered Rosa, turning her back on the twins.

"They're just jealous."

"Jealous of you?" laughed Muriel, "why you're just a little . . ."

". . . tired of you picking on us,"
finished Melody. "So why don't you
just float off and leave us alone?"

"With pleasure," said Myrtle. "You'll
never win."

And with a kick of
their tails they were
off, leaving a cloud
of sand behind
them.

The mermaids
were a little upset.

"Perhaps they're right,"
said Sula, "we will be the
youngest, and we haven't got much

20

time to practise."

But just then, Rosa let out a whoop of joy. As the water cleared, the mermaids saw a dolphin swimming towards them. Riding on its back was a beautiful mermaid.

"I can't believe you made it!" shrieked Rosa. "Sula, Jasmine, Melody, meet my cousin, Coral. She's come all the way from the South Sea."

CHAPTER 2

Stormy Waters

Sula, Jasmine and Melody swam up
to Coral to say hello. She had a mass
of dark, curly hair, which was studded
with tiny, sparkly sea stars. When she
smiled her whole face lit up.

"It's great to see you," said Rosa.

"I said I'd visit during the holidays,"

said Coral, "so here I am! I can stay until Sunday."

"Well, you've turned up at just the right time," said Rosa, and she told Coral about the carnival and the friends' plan to enter the competition.

"I'd love to join your team. If you'll have me, that is?" said Coral, looking hopefully at her cousin and her friends.

"The more the merrier," said Jasmine. Sula and Melody agreed.

"OK," said Rosa, "time for some mermaid magic then. I'm a little rusty, but I think I can remember the 'All-Change' spell. Melody, can you find me a sea horse? There should be one larking about in that seaweed over there."

"Sure thing," replied Melody, and she swam off to look.

"And we'll need some sea horns. Any idea where we can get those?"

"The Sandman has some in his shop," answered Sula. "I'll go."

"All that leaves is the main ingredient, and I always keep a sprinkle of that in here," said Rosa, tapping the tiny purse hanging from her waist. Coral and Jasmine watched as she opened it. Then all three peered inside. It was full of golden stardust, shimmering with magic.

"Aah, aah, aah . . ." began Jasmine, holding her nose as if she was about to sneeze.

"No!" screamed Rosa, snatching away her purse.

"Only joking," laughed Jasmine.

"Very funny," said Rosa, smiling weakly.

Just then, Melody returned with the sea horse. Sula

followed, trailing a string of sea horns.

"That's great," said Rosa. "Now we're ready to begin."

First she asked the mermaids to form a ring around the sea horse. Then she gave each of them a horn.

"When I say 'go', blow as hard as you can. Then swim head-to-tail in a circle. Ready?" she asked.

"Ready!" the mermaids replied.

"Go!" shouted Rosa.

Suddenly the water was filled with the rich sound of sea horns. The mermaids started to swim. They moved slowly at first, then faster

and faster, until they'd
made a whirlpool.
Gradually,
the sea
horse was
sucked in.
It spun
round
and
round
just like
a ballerina
in a music
box. Then
Rosa carefully

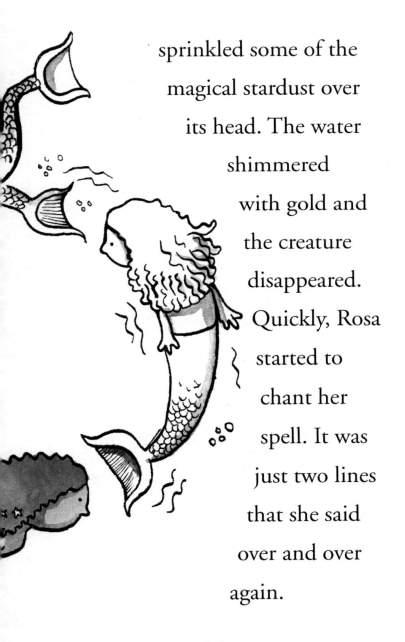

sprinkled some of the
magical stardust over
its head. The water
shimmered
with gold and
the creature
disappeared.
Quickly, Rosa
started to
chant her
spell. It was
just two lines
that she said
over and over
again.

"Inside this magic mermaid circle,

change the sea horse to a pony!"

A streak of light rushed through the swirling, shimmering water. Then, the mermaids were thrown backwards by a powerful force. Everyone waited for a pony to appear. But instead of a pony, out of the whirlpool paddled . . .

"A giant sea turtle!" gasped Sula, Melody and Jasmine at the same time. They burst into laughter.

"I did say I was a little rusty," said Rosa, going red. Still the

mermaids laughed.

"Well, I don't think it's *that* funny," said Rosa hotly. "We don't stand a chance of winning at all without the water pony."

The mermaids stopped laughing. Jasmine swam inside the grotto to look at the pearl necklace again.

"But it's so beautiful," she sighed. "What are we going to do?"

"Don't worry. I think I can help."

Everyone looked at Coral, suddenly remembering that she was there.

"Your spell didn't rhyme," she said. "*Circle* and *pony* – they don't rhyme."

"And *circle* and *turtle* do?" asked Melody.

"Well, they're near enough. Come on. What are we waiting for? You join the circle, Rosa. This time, I'll cast the spell. I've got some stardust of my own we can use."

Rosa hesitated. But Melody had

rushed off to find another sea horse, and the others were already floating in a ring. So, as soon as everything was ready, she joined the circle, the mermaids blew their horns and they made another magic whirlpool, except this time, Coral cast the spell – a spell that rhymed.

*"With horns, a whirlpool
and stardust only,
change the sea horse to a pony!"*

Flash. Smash. Out of the circle leapt a beautiful water pony. It had a pure white coat, a thick, grey mane and danced about daintily on its four shiny hooves. Stardust was stuck to his coat and it sparkled when it caught the light.

"Fantastic!" cried Sula.

"Incredible!" called Melody.

"Amazing!" shouted Jasmine.

34

"Yes, well done, Coral," said
Rosa quietly.

CHAPTER 3

Bad Sport

The mermaids led the pony to Sandy
Bottom, which was a large patch of
clear water with a soft, sandy seabed.
When they got there, the mermaids
fussed over the water pony. They
stroked his soft muzzle and ran their

fingers through his silky mane.

"What shall we call him?" asked
Sula.

"Hmmm. What about Sparkle?"
said Coral. She turned to the pony.
"Do you like that name?"

Sparkle neighed.

"Can I ride you, Sparkle?" asked
Rosa. "I'd like to practise some tricks."

Sparkle neighed again. So she
jumped onto his back and draped her
tail over one side. The others settled
down to watch.

As Sparkle started to trot, Rosa
twisted onto her tummy. Then she

brought her tail and head together and
started spinning.

"Wow!" said Jasmine.
"That's skilful."

Next, Rosa lay stretched out along
Sparkle's back. Her head
lay on his mane and
her tail covered
his. Then, with
just the slightest
flick of her body, her
head was where her tail
had been only moments
earlier. She did this
again, slowly at first,

then faster and faster, until no one could tell which end of her they were looking at – her head or her tail. Rosa had turned into a shimmering mass of scales.

"Where in the sea did you learn how to do that?" said Melody.

Rosa smiled. She knew she'd impressed them.

"Anyone else want a go?" she asked, leaping off.

"Well, if you're offering," came a voice from behind.

The mermaids turned round. Myrtle and Muriel were swimming slowly towards them.

"I meant anyone from our team," said Rosa.

"You don't mind if we stay here and watch you, then?" said Muriel. The sisters sat down on a rock, took out their sea combs and started to brush their hair.

"I'd like a go on Sparkle. It looks like fun," said Jasmine.

"Me too," said Sula. "As long as he doesn't move too fast."

So, one by one, the mermaids took a turn. Jasmine had never ridden before. She kept sliding off and each time she did, she collapsed into a heap of giggles.

It was Sula's first time at riding, too. She was a little frightened.

When Sparkle started to gallop,
she clung tightly to his mane.

Melody was a good rider.
She urged Sparkle on,
faster and faster, until
he snorted a furious flow
of hot bubbles from his nostrils and
shook his head with delight.

Finally it was Coral's turn.

"Have you ever ridden before,
Coral?" asked Sula.

"Yes," she replied. "I've got a
water pony of my own at home.
He's called Flash."

The mermaids watched Coral as she

gracefully

leapt onto Sparkle's

back. Immediately he started to trot.

Then Coral stood on her hands and

walked up and down. As she did, she arched her body, first one way and then the other. Her golden tail flashed like a firefish.

The mermaids clapped.

Then Sparkle started to gallop. This time Coral lay lengthways across his back and started to roll. Up and down she turned, faster and faster, until she let her body roll right off. Performing a flip mid-water, she

then flicked herself onto Sparkle's
back again.

The mermaids cheered.

Still on Sparkle, Coral balanced
delicately
on her
tailfin and
stretched her
arms out wide.
Then, spinning as
fast as a top, she
brought her arms
up together over her
head and pirouetted
lightly up and down.

45

Finally, with a flick of her tail she performed a triple sideflip and landed lightly on the sand.

The mermaids gasped.

"You're really talented," said Melody.

"So graceful," added Sula.

"You're the best," blurted out Jasmine. The mermaids went quiet. They were all thinking the same thing. Melody turned to Rosa.

"Rosa, would you mind if Coral rode Sparkle at the carnival too? She really is very good, and we'd have such a brilliant chance of winning if she performed her tricks as well."

Rosa's face turned pink. Her eyes pricked with tears and her mouth turned down at the corners.

"You're very good too," offered Sula.

"But she's better than me," snapped Rosa.

"Well, if that's how you feel, why doesn't Coral take my place? You don't need me any more, do you? After all, it was only my idea! Thanks, Coral. Thanks, everyone. Thanks a lot!"

And with that, she shot off before

anyone could stop her.

"Ooooooo!" giggled Muriel.

"Temper, temper," laughed Myrtle.

The mermaids looked at each other in alarm.

"What do we do now?" asked
Jasmine.

"I feel terrible," said Coral. "If only
I hadn't ridden Sparkle, Rosa wouldn't
have stormed off and everyone would
still be friends. I'll find Rosa and try
to calm her down."

"She was very cross," said Sula.
"Do you think you can?"

"I'll try," said Coral. "Anyway, it's
getting late. Let's feed Sparkle some
sweet sea pods and leave him in this
cave for the night. If we weave some
rope from seaweed and tie it across
the entrance, he can't run off. I'll meet

you all here – with Rosa, hopefully –
tomorrow morning at nine."

CHAPTER 4

Pony Trouble

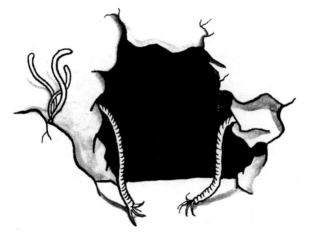

"Sparkle's gone!" cried Jasmine, as Melody and Sula swam up to the cave the following morning.

"I arrived here early to feed him and found this." She held up the seaweed rope. It was in tatters.

"Someone's ripped it apart," said Melody.

"And look at these hoof marks," said Sula. "Whoever it was has led him away."

Just then Coral swam up.

"Where's Rosa?" asked Jasmine.

"I couldn't find her," said Coral. "I went to all the usual places – Gull Rock, Sandman's Shop, Rainbow Falls, the Underwater Gardens and the Merschool. I even swam out to Splash Lagoon."

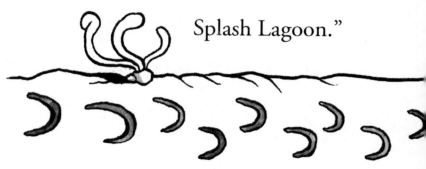

"Maybe she doesn't want to be found," said Jasmine.

"She can't still be upset," said Coral.

The mermaids went quiet.

"Sparkle's missing too," said Melody. "Someone's taken him."

"You think that Rosa did it?" asked Coral in disbelief.

The girls looked at each other.

"Well, she was very cross with us," said Sula.

"And this has ruined our chances of winning," said Jasmine.

53

"If she can't have it her way, then she doesn't want us to have it ours."

"I just don't believe Rosa would do such a thing," said Coral. "She might be angry, but she's not spiteful."

Melody swam into the cave and looked around. She examined the seaweed. There were no jagged edges.

It had been cut with something sharp.
Sparkle couldn't have done this on his
own, she thought. Jasmine was right.
Whoever did it wanted to ruin their
chances of winning the competition.
Melody was just about to swim away
when she saw something sticking out
of the sand. She picked it up, but it
was only an old sea comb.

Then she noticed something
flapping about beneath a
stone on the sea floor.

Grasping it in one hand, she called to the others.

"Look at this. Whoever took Sparkle has left a note!"

The others swam over to read it. This is what it said:

where all is dark
and nothing shines,
a SPARKLING jewel
you just might
find.

your faithful
friend,
ROSa x

"So she did take Sparkle then!" said Jasmine. "Now, rather than practising for the competition, we'll have to spend our time looking for him. 'Where all is dark and nothing shines', where could that be? I haven't a clue."

"I know," said Melody. "It's Five Fathom Forest. That place is full of sea monsters. She knows we

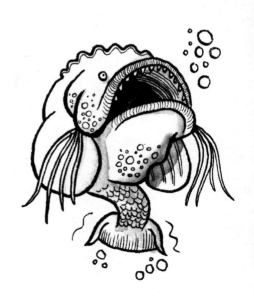

won't go in there. It's too frightening."

"Poor Sparkle," said Sula. "He must be terrified."

"Well I think we should make Rosa fetch him back. I'm not going in there to find him," said Jasmine. "Come on everyone. Let's have a splash about in the lagoon and cheer ourselves up."

But Coral didn't go. If only I hadn't turned up, she thought, Rosa wouldn't have stormed off and everyone would still be friends. It's me who should swim out to find him. It's all my fault.

CHAPTER 5

Rosa's Return

"Phew! The sun's hot today," said
Jasmine lazily, stretching out her long
blue tail on the soft sand at Splash
Lagoon. "I feel as if my scales are
about to pop."

"Take a dip," said Melody. "We can't

have you drying out. I'll come too."

"Wait," said Jasmine. "Isn't that Rosa?"

The mermaids watched as Rosa's green tail flashed towards them.

"I've come to say sorry," said Rosa, flipping out of the water and landing beside them.

"It's all very well saying sorry to us, Rosa, but what about Sparkle? I can't stop thinking of him all alone in Five Fathom Forest," said Sula. "It's cruel."

"Sparkle?" said Rosa. "I thought he was with you."

The mermaids looked confused. "But you left this," said Sula, showing Rosa the note.

"I didn't write this and I didn't take Sparkle," said Rosa. She could feel herself getting angry again. "I would never do such a thing. Where's Coral?"

"We're not sure," said Sula. "She didn't follow us here."

"Oh, no!" said Rosa. "She's probably gone to find Sparkle, but if she isn't back yet, maybe she's in trouble. We must go and find her."

Quickly the mermaids raced off to
Five Fathom Forest. Rosa entered
the cool water first. All around, thick
blades of seagrass stretched upwards
and cut out the light. As she swam,
strands clung to her scales, sea snakes
slithered across the seabed and
strange-looking fish with gaping jaws

appeared at every turn. Every now and then the rotten remains of a wrecked boat or some drowned piece of junk loomed in front of her. Covered in barnacles and dripping with seaweed, they looked like huge sea monsters. Rosa shivered. Then she noticed a flash of gold. "Come on, everyone, I can see something," she called.

"Help me! Help!" cried a voice.

Rosa swam forwards quickly. Her heart was beating hard. The others followed.

"Thank goodness you're here," said Coral. "My tail's caught in this old net. I found Sparkle wandering around in here and was leading him back when it happened. He's been keeping me company, haven't you, boy?" Sparkle nuzzled Coral's ear.

Carefully, Rosa freed Coral's tail from the net. "Ouch!" said Coral. "It's quite painful."

"Come on," said Rosa. "Let's get out of here. Hold on to Sparkle's mane. I'll lead the way."

Finally the mermaids found their way back. They went straight to Sandy Bottom, where Rosa went to find some seagrass to feed Sparkle.

"Thank goodness Rosa found you," said Sula.

"But if Rosa didn't take Sparkle, who did?" said Melody.

"Whoever wrote that note wanted us to think it was her. But why would anyone do such a thing?"

Just then, Myrtle and Muriel swam up. They stopped suddenly, looking surprised.

"What's wrong?" asked Rosa, her hands full of juicy seagrass.

"Nothing," said Myrtle.

Rosa tried to feed Sparkle, but he backed away and kept his jaws firmly shut. She felt his body. He was trembling.

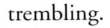

"You don't know anything about Sparkle disappearing, do you?" asked Rosa suspiciously.

"Coral went to look for him but became tangled in an old net.

I found her in a terrible state."

"No, why should we?' asked Muriel.

"It's just that . . ." but before Rosa could finish, Muriel carried on,

"That's typical! Blame us! After the way your friends treated you yesterday, Rosa, I'm surprised you bothered to go to Five Fathom Forest to help."

Rosa looked puzzled.

"I didn't say they were in Five Fathom Forest, Muriel. How do you know that's where they were?" she said.

As she spoke, Coral picked up the comb from the sand.

"I knew I'd seen this before," she said. "It's yours, isn't it, Muriel? You dropped it when you set Sparkle loose."

But before they got any answers, Muriel snatched away the comb, and together with Myrtle, turned on her tail and swam off.

Now it was the mermaids' turn to look surprised.

"They're big trouble, those two," said Jasmine. "I'm so sorry we blamed you, Rosa."

"No, it's me who should be sorry," said Rosa. "I was so angry, I'm not surprised you thought I'd want to ruin everything. You're right, Coral is the best, so she should perform too.

Now the carnival is tomorrow and we've hardly practised."

"So," said Coral, "what are we waiting for?"

CHAPTER 6
Party Time

It was the day of the carnival. The sea folk of Mermaid Bay had gathered outside Crystal Grotto and were waiting for all the teams to arrive. The procession was to lead through Rock Theatre, past the Merschool and the

Underwater Gardens, under Rainbow Falls and finish at King Neptune's Palace. There, King Neptune would decide which team was to win the prize – the glorious, the splendid, the most magnificent pearl necklace anyone had ever seen! Excitement buzzed through the water.

Rosa, Coral, Jasmine, Melody and Sula, or 'The Waterbabes' as they were called, were outside the grotto too. They had dressed up and were keen to begin.

Coral was wearing a tiara made from
golden sea bracken and decorated with
tiny mother-of-pearl beads. Rosa wore
a halter-neck top made from shiny
fish scales. Sula had given everyone a

colourful gauze scarf to hold. Melody
had carefully braided silver thread into
her hair, and Jasmine wore a top made
from golden seaweed. It had trailing
strands that floated outwards in the

water every time she moved. And the
mermaids had smartened up Sparkle,
too. They had braided his mane and
tail with gold ribbons,
and brushed his coat
until it shone.
At last the
procession began.
Rosa sat on Sparkle.
She amazed the
crowd with
her skilful
tailspins, backflips and
handsprings, while the four other
mermaids twisted and twirled about.

After Rosa,
Coral
took her
turn. Her
pirouettes
were
mesmerising.

So mesmerising, in
fact, that no one noticed the two older
mermaids, Myrtle and Muriel, arguing
beneath Rainbow Falls.

"I told you we should have
practised," said Myrtle.

"It's all your fault," said Muriel. "If
only you weren't so clumsy."

"Me clumsy?" replied Myrtle.
"You're the one with two left fins."

"Oh, I'm going home," said Myrtle,
and she stormed off.

Finally, the procession approached
King Neptune's Palace, where a new
crowd was waiting. Rosa was having

such fun she had to pinch herself to
make sure she wasn't dreaming. When
King Neptune himself appeared, the
crowd cheered. After a few moments
he held up his hand. Everybody
went quiet.

"Sea folk of Mermaid Bay," he
bellowed from behind his fluffy, white
beard, "welcome to Mermaid Bay's
tenth Midsummer Carnival."

The crowd cheered again.

"The time has come for me to
present this wonderful prize."

He held up the necklace for
everyone to see. The crowd gasped.

"And, I think you'll all agree, that there was one team that stood out from all the rest. They were skilful, dazzling, and, most importantly, looked as if they were having lots of fun."

The mermaids held their breath.

"And so, it is with great pleasure that I award the prize to the youngest contestants here today – 'The Waterbabes'."

Coral, Rosa, Melody, Jasmine and Sula turned somersaults in the water. The crowd laughed at their delight.

Then, as King Neptune handed them the necklace, the mermaids raised it above their heads.

It shone almost as brightly as their faces.

"We did it!" they shouted. The
crowd cheered.

"Now let the celebrations begin!"
King Neptune cried. The doors to
the palace were flung open. Sea
creatures carrying platters piled high

with delicious food swam out. Music filled the air, everyone danced and the mermaids, full of their success, celebrated long into the night.

The following day, it was time for Coral to go home. The mermaids gathered at Crystal Grotto, together with Sparkle, to say goodbye.

"We've got something we want you to have, Coral," said Rosa, and she held out the pearl necklace.

Coral gasped. "I couldn't," she said, "it's yours."

"No," said
Rosa, "it's yours.
You found
Sparkle. You
didn't give up on
us. You helped us
to win."

The others
nodded in agreement.

Coral took the necklace and
tied it round her neck. It looked
magnificent.

"Thank you," she said. Then she
gave each of the mermaids a hug and
swam off.

"Goodbye," the mermaids shouted,
waving as she swam into the distance,
"come and visit again soon!"

When Coral had finally
disappeared, Jasmine turned to
the others.

"Now, before we go home, shouldn't

we turn Sparkle back into a sea horse?
It's been a wonderful adventure for
him, but we can't keep him like this
forever. Can you do it, Rosa?"

"OK. At least I know what to do
this time," she said confidently.

So, after each mermaid had given
Sparkle a hug, once again, they
formed a ring around the creature.
Then, blowing their horns, the friends
started to move around him, slowly
at first, then faster and faster.
As soon as Sparkle began to spin, Rosa
threw in some stardust and started to
chant her spell.

"With music, dust and magical force,
change Sparkle back into a sea horse."

Flash. Smash. The water cleared.
Rosa held her breath, and out of the
pool came . . .

"A SEA MONSTER!"
screamed Rosa. "Quick,
let's get out of here."
But the other
mermaids weren't going
anywhere. They were
laughing at her again.
"Let's go. Now!" insisted

90

Rosa, looking worried.

Still the mermaids laughed.

"It's only me, Rosa," giggled
Jasmine, pulling a huge pile of
seaweed from her head.

Sure enough, there was the tiny
sea horse beside
her. The
spell had
worked,
after all.
And this
time, Rosa
laughed
too.

Here's a sneak preview
of another exciting
mermaid mystery

A water fairy,
a beautiful love story
and a legend of lost
treasure.

CHAPTER 1

Friends Forever

It was a chilly autumn morning in Mermaid Bay. Jasmine, Melody and Sula were at Gull Rock waiting for their friend, Rosa, to arrive.

"Listen. This will make you laugh," said Jasmine. "Why *did* the lobster blush?"

"I don't know," said Melody. "Why did the lobster blush?"

"Because the sea-weed!"

"That's revolting," cried Sula, laughing.

"It's silly," said Melody. "Everyone knows lobsters can't blush."

"OK. I'll tell you another," said Jasmine, determined to make Melody laugh. "What's another name for a mermaid?"

Melody and Sula shook their heads.

"A deep-SHE fish!"

This time they both laughed.

"There! Made you smile," said Jasmine brightly. She loved to make her friends laugh.

"Where *has* Rosa got to?" said Melody. "It's not like her to be late."

"There she is," said Sula, pointing at something green, flashing through the water. Swiftly Rosa reached the rock.

"You're late," said Melody.

"I'm sorry. Follow me and I'll show you why," Rosa replied.

To find out what happens, buy your copy today.